For Amy, Mum and my super brother, Andy.

ORCHARD BOOKS
Carmelite House, 50 Victoria Embankment, London EC4Y 0DZ
First published in 2016 by Orchard Books • ISBN 978 1 40833 728 8
Text and illustrations © Matt Robertson 2016
The right of Matt Robertson to be identified as the author and illustrator of this work has
been asserted by him in accordance with the Copyright, Designs and Patents Act, 1988.
A CIP catalogue record for this book is available from the British Library.
1 3 5 7 9 10 8 6 4 2 • Printed in China • Orchard Books
An imprint of Hachette Children's Group
Part of the Watts Publishing Group Limited
An Hachette UK company
www.hachette.co.uk

SUPER STAN

Matt Robertson

ORCHARD

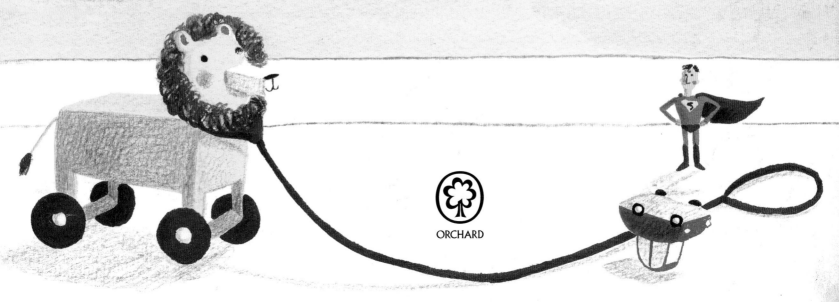

Jack and Stan were brothers.

JACK

They were very different.

STAN

Stan could always run FASTER...

...throw FURTHER...

... and jump HIGHER.

Oh, and Stan could also . . .

...FLY!

Whenever Jack did something ordinary,

Stan did something EXTRAordinary.

Whenever Jack did
something good,

Stan did something AMAZING!

The whole world thought
Stan was super . . .

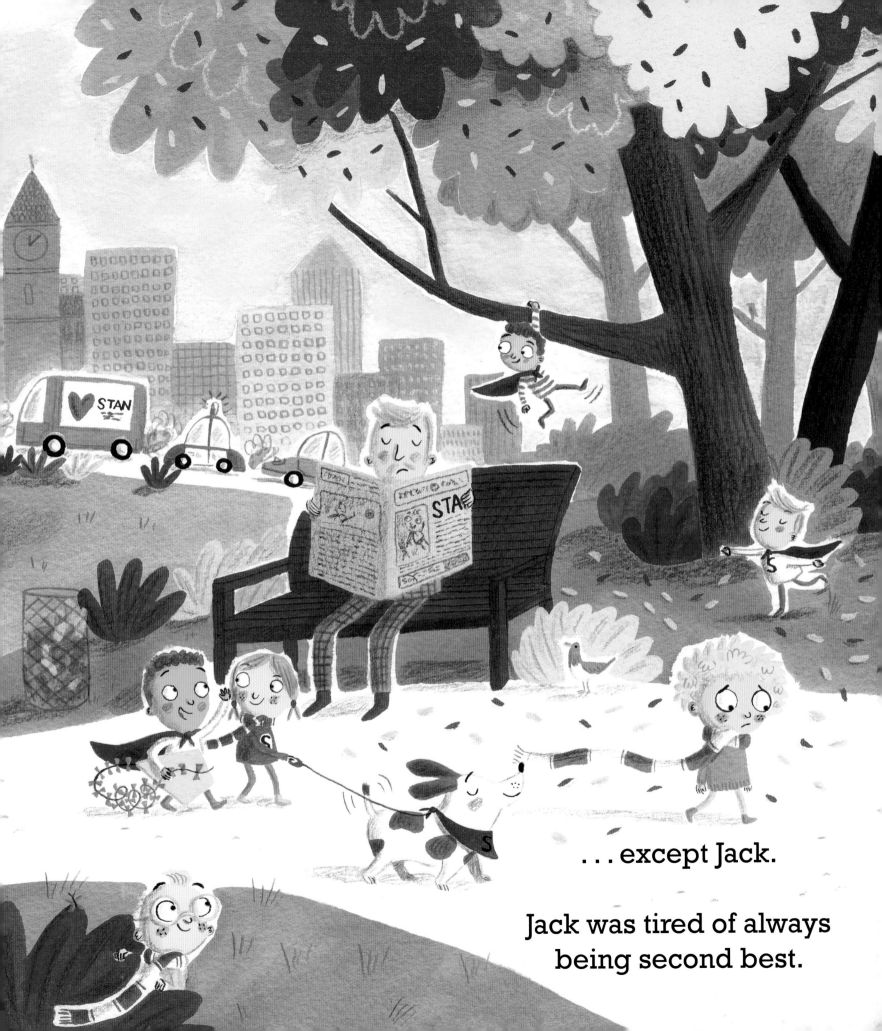

. . . except Jack.

Jack was tired of always
being second best.

On Jack's birthday,
his special treat was
a trip to the zoo.

He didn't want anything
to spoil his day.

"Please don't ruin my birthday treat, Stan," said Jack.

But Stan was far too excited to listen.

Before long, Stan was racing the CHEETAHS...

...wrestling a

LION...

...and playing with the GIRAFFES.

Everyone clapped and cheered . . .

. . . except Jack.

"This was supposed to be
MY special day,"
Jack thought sadly.

But then Jack heard a sound.

Stan sniffed . . .
his lip wobbled . . .
and then he let out a SUPER scream.

WAAAAAAAAA

The crying got
LOUDER and
LOUDER.

Nobody knew
what was wrong
... except Jack.

Because, after all,
he was Stan's big
brother.

As quick as a flash,
Jack sprang into action!

And just . . .

in the nick . . .

of TIME . . . .

...JACK

SAVED THE

DAY!

After all, that's what big brothers do.

Stan stopped crying and gave Jack a

SUPER hug.

Jack felt like a real super hero!

And from that day on, Jack and Stan were
SUPER BROTHERS!

THE SUPER BROTHERS